THE SEVEN AND THE RACING DRIVER

Enjoy another thrilling adventure with the Secret Seven. They are Peter, Janet, Pam, Colin, George, Jack, Barbara and, of course, Scamper the Spaniel.

When a noisy, shiny sports car draws in to Old Mill Farm, Peter can scarcely believe his ears or eyes. And when he learns that the driver is the organizer of a forthcoming motor race, he and the rest of the Secret Seven can't wait to visit the track. But when, on the day before the race, the favourite for the title disappears, the Seven are suspicious that all is not as it seems.

The Seven and the Racing Driver

A new adventure of the
characters created by
Enid Blyton, told by Evelyne
Lallemand, translated by
Anthea Bell

Illustrated by Maureen Bradley

KNIGHT BOOKS
Hodder and Stoughton

Copyright © Librairie Hachette 1982
First published in France as *Les Sept à 200 à l'heure*
English Language translation copyright © Hodder & Stoughton
Ltd 1987
Illustrations copyright © Hodder & Stoughton Ltd 1987

First published in Great Britain by Knight Books 1987

British Library Cataloguing in Publication Data

Lallemand, Evelyne
  The seven and the racing driver : a new
  adventure of the characters created by
  Enid Blyton.
  I. Title   II. Bradley, Maureen   III. Blyton,
  Enid   IV. Les sept à 200 à l'heure. *English*
843′.914[J]   PZ7

  ISBN 0-340-40853-7

Printed and bound in Great Britain for
Hodder and Stoughton Paperbacks, a
division of Hodder and Stoughton Ltd.,
Mill Road, Dunton Green, Sevenoaks,
Kent (Editorial Office: 47 Bedford
Square, London WC1B 3DP) by
Cox & Wyman, Reading

CONTENTS

Chapter One

EXCITEMENT AHEAD!

Peter was up in the loft of the barn in his father's farmyard, reading an adventure story, when a car shot in through the farm gates and stopped dead with a squeal of its brakes.

'I *say*!' breathed Peter, looking down at it.

For it wasn't just any old car. It was a big, shiny, beautiful sports car, with a powerful engine – not the sort of thing Peter often saw in the village where he and his family lived.

'Super!' he said to himself as he closed his book and climbed down the ladder from the loft.

As he went towards the splendid-looking sports car, a tall man got out of it. 'Hallo!' he said, giving the boy his hand. 'I'm John Lorimer!'

'Hallo, sir!' said Peter, shaking hands. 'Er . . . I'm afraid you've come to the wrong place. This isn't a garage. It's Old Mill Farm.'

'Yes, I know!' said the man, smiling. 'I can tell the difference between a cow and a petrol pump . . .

I think!' And he burst out laughing. It was an infectious sort of laugh, and next moment Peter was joining in.

Hearing his son laughing and talking to a visitor, Peter's father, who had been working inside the stables, came out into the yard. The first thing he saw was the car, and then he spotted Mr Lorimer and Peter standing beside it. He went over to them, wondering what on earth was up!

'Good afternoon,' he said. Mr Lorimer immediately stopped laughing, introduced himself to Peter's father, and then explained why he had come.

What Mr Lorimer had to say sounded more exciting than any book! And listening to him, Peter forgot all about the adventure story he had left at the top of the ladder. He drank in every word. Goodness! This was simply thrilling.

Next day Peter summoned the Secret Seven to meet in their usual place, the garden-shed. Everybody came – including Scamper the golden spaniel, who settled down comfortably at the children's feet on a bit of old rug.

Peter opened the meeting, and told the others all about the car and how he had seen it arrive. He went into a full description, even imitating the noise of its powerful engine, and squealing to show the others how its brakes sounded when it drew up in the farmyard, interrupting him in the middle of his book. In fact, he described the sports car in such detail that Colin, for one, began to get rather impatient.

'That's all very well, Peter,' he said, 'but when are you coming to the point?'

'Yes, what was the driver of this sports car after?' said Barbara. 'Do stop keeping us in suspense, Peter!'

'All right, all *right*,' said Peter. 'I'm just *coming* to the point – wait till you hear it!'

'That's exactly what we are doing,' Colin said.

But Peter wasn't to be hurried. He described the way he had thought the driver must have called at the farm by mistake, and how his father came along to see what their visitor wanted. 'And the driver's name is Lorimer,' he added.

The others looked blank. They couldn't see what was so exciting about that! However, it did seem as if they were getting to the facts at last, as Jack pointed out. 'Let's hear the rest of it, Peter,' he said impatiently. 'Give us something to chew on!'

Catching these words, Scamper sat up all of a sudden looking very lively and hopeful, as if he expected a nice bowl of dog's-meat!

'No, no, Scamper!' said Janet, patting the spaniel. '*You're* not getting something to chew on – anyway, you've just had your dinner, you greedy dog! Jack didn't mean it like that.'

Scamper settled down again like a good dog.

'Right!' said Peter. 'This Mr Lorimer – Mr John Lorimer,' he added, speaking slowly and solemnly, so as to impress the others, 'this Mr John Lorimer has come to our part of the country to organize the Malling Castle Motor Race!'

'My word!' said Colin. 'How exciting!'

'Wait a minute – I heard about the proposal to have a big motor-racing event at Malling,' said Jack. 'But wasn't it turned down by the local council last year?'

'Well, they've passed it now, anyway,' said Peter. 'And the race is going to be next month!'

'How super!' said Colin. 'A real motor race – with real Formula 1 cars, practically as long as aeroplanes

10

and with enormous great wheels! It'll be much better than watching motor racing on television!'

'I don't know *much* about motor racing,' admitted Pam, 'but I still don't see what this Mr Lorimer was doing at your father's farm, Peter! What's the connection with the motor race?'

'Simple! He wanted to buy some bales of straw,' Peter explained.

'Oh, now I see! Yes, they use bales of straw for protection round the track, don't they?' said Colin.

'That's right,' Peter said. 'He ordered two lorry-loads of straw. And he told us they were going to build stands for spectators, and pits for the cars, and all sorts of things!'

'It sounds like a really big event!' said Jack happily. He was very interested in motor racing – so were the other boys!

'Three cheers for the Malling Castle Motor Race!' cried George. 'Hip, hip, hurray!' And all four boys cheered heartily and started dancing round and round in their excitement.

The girls were feeling rather left out. 'Doesn't take much to make *them* happy, does it?' said Barbara rather sharply, looking at the boys prancing about.

'Just look at them!' said Pam. 'Fooling about like that! They'll tread on Scamper if they're not careful! *I* don't see what's so special about a motor race.'

'Well, while they're all off looking at racing cars, we can have the garden shed to ourselves and plan

a special party,' said Janet. 'I think that would be much more fun!'

'I don't!' said Barbara firmly. 'Suppose they went and had some sort of adventure without us?'

'I tell you what!' said Pam. 'We could go and look for an adventure of our own, and have one without the boys for once!'

'Good idea!' agreed Janet.

And the three girls were just about to leave the shed and the whooping, prancing boys, when Peter calmed down a bit and mentioned the name of the driver who was favourite to win the race. They stopped dead and looked at him enquiringly.

'That's what I said – Mike Lee!' Peter repeated. 'Mike Lee himself will be in Malling next month!'

'Ooh – Mike Lee!' breathed Barbara, astonished.

'There was a photograph of him in the paper last week,' said Janet.

'He's awfully good-looking!' said Pam. 'Dark, with blue eyes. And they say he isn't twenty yet, although he's already such a famous racing driver!'

All three girls turned back into the shed. Suddenly they felt much more interested in the race than before.

Peter had been lucky to get the great news so soon – it wasn't till next day that everyone could read about it in the local newspapers, which printed several photographs of racing cars and their drivers, and had a long interview with the famous driver Mike Lee. Pam and Barbara were fascinated, and read the interview many times.

Over the next week, the Seven met Mr Lorimer several times in the market town not far from their village. Peter introduced his friends to the race organizer, and after that he always gave them a friendly wave when they happened to pass each other. The market town, and all the villages round about, were already much busier than usual because of the race. You could see vans painted in bright colours driving about, advertising different kinds of petrol or tyres, and a team of workmen came to

13

prepare the race track. They were staying at the Station Hotel in the market town. The Manor House Hotel, a very nice place in the country not far from the Seven's village, was busily reserving rooms for the drivers and the top newspaper reporters who would be coming to write about the race, and other local hotels were to put up a great many maintenance men and other people involved in the organization of the event.

On Monday, two articulated lorries turned up at the Old Mill Farm to collect the straw Mr Lorimer had ordered. It took three hours to load up all the

bales, and then they drove off again.

The great day itself was less than three weeks off now, and the whole countryside was thrilled to have such a big motor-racing event in the area. There were posters up on walls and hoardings, and streamers and bunting hung across the roads. It was quite a change for what was usually a very quiet part of the country – and the Secret Seven were as excited as everyone else!

Two days after the straw had been collected, Peter decided it was time to go and take a look at the new Malling Circuit. He had asked Mr Lorimer if that was allowed, and the race organizer said that it would be quite all right, since they were friends of his. The others all thought the expedition was a good idea, so soon the Seven were on their bicycles, and riding along the road to Malling. It was quite a straight main road as far as the foot of the hill on which the Castle stood, but they knew that the little road up the hill itself was a steep, winding one, so they were prepared to push their bikes the last part of the way.

If they could go along it at all, that is – for much to their surprise, as they turned off the main road and came to the first bend of the small road leading uphill to Malling Castle, they found a large, striped red and white barrier across it, with a motor cyclist guarding it, his motor-bike propped on its stand beside him.

Chapter Two

THE MALLING CIRCUIT

'Stop!' said the uniformed motor cyclist. 'You can't use this road.'

Peter put the brakes on his bike, and so did the six others.

'We've come to look at the circuit,' he explained.

'Sorry, that's not allowed,' the motor cyclist said firmly.

'Oh, but we're expected all right!' Pam said, giving him a nice smile. 'Mr Lorimer himself said we could go up there.'

'Mr Lorimer?' said the man. 'Who's he?'

'Why, he's the chief organizer of the race!' Jack told him. 'The boss of the whole show!'

'The organizer, eh?' said the motor cyclist, scratching his chin. 'Oh, well . . . I suppose you can go in then, but you'll have to leave your bicycles here and go up on foot.'

Since they'd expected to push their bikes part of the way in any case, the Seven didn't mind at all –

and a moment later they were the other side of the barrier.

'Hey, look!' said Colin when they'd gone a little way. 'They've widened the road, haven't they?'

'Only here,' Barbara noticed. 'It's as narrow as ever higher up.' And she pointed to the thin ribbon of road winding its way up the hill.

'I know what it is,' said George. 'They've widened this part of the road for the start of the race.'

'Yes, that must be the idea,' Jack agreed. 'And look, over there! I can see some workmen putting up tiers of seats.'

'And those must be the pits where the cars will be parked before the start,' said Pam, pointing to large wooden enclosures which had been built to the left of the seating. By now she knew a lot more about motor racing than she had before Mr Lorimer called at Old Mill Farm.

Suddenly the children heard loud music – so loud that Janet uttered a little squeal of surprise.

'Testing for sound . . . testing for sound!' bellowed a voice over the giant loudspeakers hanging from wooden posts at the four corners of the newly constructed esplanade.

'Testing . . . sound . . . ' the voice went on, and then it was interrupted by a tremendous crackle!

'Haven't got it quite right yet, have they?' said Colin, laughing.

Next moment the music came back again, but not nearly so loud this time. In fact it almost sounded pleasant. 'That's a bit better!' said Janet, uncovering her ears.

'Well, come on!' Peter told the others. 'Let's carry on with our tour of the race track! First the start, then the gradient.'

'The what?' said Janet.

'The hilly bit,' Peter informed his sister. 'You call it a gradient in motor racing.' He wasn't quite sure of this, but there was no need to let the others know that. 'Ladies and gentlemen, kindly follow your guide!' he added.

They climbed on for about half a mile. The winding little road here was just the same as usual. There

18

was a steep drop towards the fields at the foot of the hill on one side of it, and the hill went on rising on the other. The brambles that grew by the roadside were in flower, and Pam was pleased to see that there would be a good crop of blackberries that year.

The children hadn't met a living soul since they left the esplanade where the race would start. And then, as they went round a bend, a strong and not particularly pleasant smell, blown towards them by the wind, told them that road-work was in progress a little further up.

'Ugh! What a horrible smell!' said Janet, holding her nose.

'It's tar. They must be reinforcing the surface of the road,' said Colin.

'That's not surprising,' said George. 'There were holes in this road anyway, and they got a lot worse in the cold weather last winter.'

'Yes, and if you went over one of those holes at a hundred miles an hour, it'd not be fun!' said Jack. 'You'd go right over that steep drop, or crash into the hillside.'

They could already hear the sound of machinery working. A little further on they saw the place where workmen were resurfacing the road. Parts of it were thickly covered with a layer of steaming tar. They avoided the tar by going off the road itself and into the wood which covered the hillside just there, and they found a pathway which brought them back to the road itself above the next bend.

It took them another twenty minutes to reach Malling Castle, avoiding all the patches of fresh tar on the road. Bales of straw had been put in place by the roadside, and there was a white line painted down the middle.

At last the towers of Malling Castle appeared above the treetops, and when the children reached

the castle building they found Mr Lorimer outside it. He was very busy, holding a megaphone and shouting directions to three men perched on ladders. They were hanging blue and yellow draperies over the front of the seating which had been put up for people to watch the finish of the race. But he wasn't too busy to come over and say hallo to the Seven when he saw them arrive.

'How do you like the look of that blue and yellow colour combination?' he asked the children, smiling cheerfully.

'It's pretty,' said Barbara.

'Yes. They're the colours we've chosen for the Malling Castle Motor Race,' said Mr Lorimer. 'See that big medallion?'

He was pointing to a large yellow circle with a racing-car's wheel painted on it in blue. The three workmen were just hauling it up into place above the seating, to add the finishing touch to the decorations. 'Stop!' Mr Lorimer shouted through his megaphone. 'That's it, perfect!' He turned back to the children and asked, 'Well, what do you think?'

'Great!' said Peter enthusiastically.

'This is where the winning driver will be handed his prize at the end of the first Malling Castle Motor Race,' said Mr Lorimer. 'I've asked one of the local landowners, called Mr Fitzwilliam, to present the prize.'

'Oh, we know Mr Fitzwilliam quite well!' Peter

told him. 'He lives at the Hall, not far from my father's farm.'

'Yes, and as he owns the land on which we're constructing the track, he seemed to be the right person to make the presentation,' said Mr Lorimer.

'I bet Mike Lee wins the race!' said Pam, dancing up and down with excitement.

'He certainly stands a good chance,' said the organizer. 'But he'll have some pretty stiff competition, you know. Pedro Gonzalez, the Spanish driver, will be taking part in the race, and Angelo Giannini, the Italian, and I mustn't forget the American driver Jimmy Curtis!'

'Goodness! Is Jimmy Curtis going to be in the race too?' asked Jack.

'I say! That *is* competition and no mistake!' agreed Colin.

'Jimmy Curtis won one of the Grand Prix races on the Continent this year, didn't he?' asked Peter, very interested.

'That's right,' said Mr Lorimer. 'He's a very famous name. He was world champion four years running, you know, until last year when young Lee just pipped him at the post!'

'When will the drivers be arriving?' asked Janet eagerly.

'Next week,' Mr Lorimer told her. 'Malling is a new circuit, so they'll need time to get to know it. They have to be familiar with every little bump, every turn in the road and every bit of the straight sections. A good racing driver could almost drive with his eyes closed once he's acquainted with the track.'

'How clever!' breathed Pam admiringly.

And then the children were asked to move, because workmen with paint guns were marking a long, vertical, white line between the wooden stands. 'The finishing line,' said Mr Lorimer. And all the children wondered which of the four world-famous drivers he had mentioned would be the one to pass it first.

The afternoon was nearly over when the Seven went down the road to the bottom of the hill again. They had been very careful not to walk on the patches of fresh tar as they went up, and they were surprised to see that somebody else hadn't been so thoughtful.

'What a shame!' said George. 'Look – there are footmarks everywhere! You'd almost think someone had done it on purpose.'

'They did,' said Colin. 'The footprints are going in all directions. If I caught whoever stamped about on the sticky tar like that . . . '

'It looks to me as if you can!' said Barbara, pointing a little way downhill. There were Jack's annoying little sister Susie and her great friend Binkie.

'Those two little pests!' said Jack crossly. 'I suppose we might have known it, just from looking at the size of the footprints!'

'I bet Susie was listening at the keyhole when you told your parents you were going up to Malling Castle,' Janet guessed.

'She really is *awful*!' groaned Jack. Susie was a great trial to him! And then he stopped dead. 'Well, really! The cheek of it!' he added. 'See what they've done? They've taken away some of the bales of straw.'

'And they're using them to build a pyramid!' said Peter, equally horrified.

'Down with Susie and Binkie!' shouted Colin, shaking his fist.

And the Seven all began running towards the two little girls.

Seeing Jack and his friends bearing down on them, Susie and Binkie let out squeals of alarm, and ran off as fast as their legs would carry them. They didn't stop to ask what the Secret Seven wanted – they had a very good idea, and were on their bicycles and cycling away within seconds!

Peter tried snatching up his own bike to follow them, and then found he couldn't move it! 'Sabotage!' he said furiously. His back wheel had been firmly tied to the front wheel of the bicycle next to his.

'The little horrors!' cried Jack. All seven bikes had been tied together in the same way! 'They'll be sorry for this,' he added grimly.

A few feet away from the children, the motor cyclist guard was smiling with amusement! But the Seven didn't feel it was at all funny. Trust Susie and Binkie to go sticking their oar in! It was going to spoil everything if *they* started taking an interest in the Malling Castle Motor Race too, thought Jack gloomily, but that was his little sister all over!

'Don't let it bother you,' said Peter, reading his friend's thoughts. 'If we just take no notice of Susie and Binkie, they'll soon get tired of trying to annoy us. Personally, I intend to enjoy these holidays and the motor race, and I shan't let anyone stop me!'

'Hear, hear!' said the rest of the Seven in chorus.

Chapter Three

THE DRIVERS ARRIVE

Next week the racing drivers who were actually going to take part in the Malling Castle Motor Race began to arrive.

Jack was the first to see a racing car. One morning he went to the baker's for his mother, and, coming back with a new loaf and half a dozen bread rolls, he saw it being pulled down the village street on a trailer drawn by a large saloon car. He ran over to get a closer look.

The racing car was very, very long, with most impressive wheels. The back wheels actually rose above its sparkling bodywork. There were four silencers looking like organ pipes as they emerged from beneath the horizontal stabilizer – the car went at such speed that without that, it would have left the road and taken to the air like a supersonic plane!

Other cars turned up over the next few days. They all looked just as impressive – not at all like the ordinary cars in which the people of the local coun-

tryside drove about. Soon the Manor House Hotel, where the most important people involved in the race were staying, seemed as if it were the centre of the whole motor-racing world.

George, Colin, Jack and Peter kept walking past the hotel, trying to recognize famous faces. When it was fine, and there were tables on the terrace outside it, they even ventured to stroll among them, pretending to be hotel guests, looking at the reporters and photographers and those racing drivers who had already turned up. But the most interesting drivers were the last to arrive. None of the Seven had set eyes on Mike Lee or Jimmy Curtis yet, but the boys did hear people mentioning those two names as if they were great rivals.

'One of them's sure to win!' said Peter confidently, and his friends agreed with him.

Practice began on the Tuesday of the week when the race was to be held, and all the Seven went to Malling Castle to watch. They weren't the only ones either! There were dozens of keen fans at the race track.

Some of them had even arrived the night before, and were planning to camp near the circuit until the great event took place. They had put up tents in a field near the track. Nobody in these parts had ever seen such a crowd about the place before! It was like a Bank Holiday – there were even stalls selling hot dogs and hamburgers. The racing cars were in the pits, their engines turning over; orders were shouted over the loudspeakers; men in overalls were running here, there and everywhere. It was a cheerful scene of noise and movement.

Peter and the rest of the Seven made straight for the cars themselves.

'I can't see Mike Lee!' Pam kept saying, 'I wonder where he is!'

'Perhaps he hasn't arrived yet,' said Barbara. She was longing to see the famous racing driver too.

'Yes, he has!' Jack told her. 'They mentioned it on the regional TV programme last night.'

'Look, that's Gonzalez's pit,' said Colin, pointing to one of the pits as they passed it.

'España,' Barbara read out loud, looking at the notice on it.

'*España, país del sol y del as del volante*,' said a dark little man, grinning at her. He had spots of grease on his overalls.

Barbara's eyes widened in surprise. 'Er . . . sorry, me no understand,' she stammered. 'Me no speak Spanish, only English!'

'Honestly, Barbara, what *do* you think you're doing, speaking baby-talk like that?' said George. 'He may be Spanish but he's not an idiot, you know!'

'Thanks for the compliment!' said the little man in perfectly good English, though with a strong foreign accent. And turning to Barbara, who had gone bright red at George's remark, he added, 'All I said was: Spain, country of the sun and the King of the steering-wheel.'

'I say – are you Pedro Gonzalez, then?' asked Peter.

The little man roared with laughter, went over to a box of tools and took out a large adjustable spanner. 'No, no! I'm just his mechanic! King of the tool-box, that's me!' he said, waving his spanner about.

'Well said!' remarked someone behind the little group of children who had gathered around the mechanic. The Seven turned round and saw a handsome man with a sunburnt face, wearing spotless white overalls and smiling at them.

He introduced himself. 'I'm Pedro Gonzalez, and

29

this is Juan, my faithful right-hand man!'

Feeling quite overawed, the children shook hands with the famous racing driver.

'Well, time to start work!' he said cheerfully, adjusting his helmet.

'Good luck!' said Peter, as he settled into the narrow seat of the car. Juan gave the children a friendly wave and disappeared head first into the insides of the engine, to check it over for the last time.

'I like Pedro Gonzalez!' said Barbara, as the Seven moved away.

'I still can't see Mike Lee's car,' said Pam dolefully. She was searching for something to show where the English driver would be in the pits.

'Well, never mind – look, there's Jimmy Curtis anyway,' Peter told her, pointing. And he set off towards that part of the pits. Three red letters on a white background, saying USA, had shown him where to find the former world champion.

The rest of the Seven followed him.

'There's Curtis!' whispered Colin, in awe.

'Where? Where?' asked Barbara.

'Over there behind the car, reading a newspaper.'

'Are you sure that's him?' asked Jack incredulously.

'Perfectly sure,' George told him. 'I recognize him – they had his photograph in the local paper last week, don't you remember?'

Suddenly a red-haired and very fat man came into the pit. He seemed to be in an extremely bad temper.

'You know something? They put them right beside us!' he said angrily. 'It's scandalous!'

'Oh, come along, Bob! They have a draw for the pit numbers, don't they?' said Curtis, without raising his eyes from his newspaper.

'Yeah, sure – and they fix that draw!' said the red-haired man drily. At that moment he noticed the Seven standing there and listening to the conversation. 'Hey, you kids got no business here!' he said roughly. 'Go on, get out!'

'With pleasure!' said Peter, sarcastically, leading the Seven away again. They were all rather annoyed – they hadn't been doing anything except look at the drivers, and they'd been careful not to get in anyone's way!

'What a beast that man is!' said Peter between his teeth.

'And Curtis didn't turn a hair, either!' said Barbara. She thought that as a couple, they were very different from Pedro Gonzalez and Juan!

'There!' cried Pam all of a sudden.

She had stopped dead. Mike Lee was less than ten metres away, looking splendid in sky-blue over-alls.

'Isn't he good-looking?' breathed Barbara. 'Even

better-looking than in his photographs!'

Mr Lorimer was talking to him, and there was a very pretty young woman with the two men.

'That's Mike Lee's fiancée,' said George. 'They're going to get married in two months' time. It said in the paper.'

'Mind your backs!' said a cheerful voice quite close to the Seven. They looked round, and then jumped out of the way. A man in sky-blue dungarees wanted to get past them. He was pushing a heavy trolley, loaded up with tools and spare parts.

'You might as well lend a hand, instead of standing there staring!' he added good-humouredly, grinning at the children. 'Here – catch this!'

And that was how the Seven got into Mike Lee's pit, along with his friendly mechanic Johnny. Mike Lee himself soon joined them, and Johnny, who had quickly learnt all the children's names, made the introductions.

'Mike, meet the Secret Seven,' he said cheerfully. 'Seven, meet Mike Lee!'

Pam could hardly believe their luck! She went bright red when the young racing driver shook hands. Then they were introduced to his fiancée, Marianne. She seemed extremely nice too, and smiled at all the children in a very friendly way. Mike Lee insisted on buying all the Seven some orange squash before they went home to the village for their lunch. They were all determined to come

back straight afterwards – because the actual practice was to start in the afternoon! The really exciting part of these holidays was about to begin.

Chapter Four

PRACTICE SESSIONS

When the Seven got back to the circuit, they heard voices over the loudpseakers counting seconds, giving the signal to start, saying what cars were going on the track, and so on. 'The Lotus to the start,' they were announcing. 'Lotus to the start. Countdown about to begin! Ten, nine, eight, seven, six, five . . . '

Car engines were roaring everywhere, and mechanics were running in all directions.

'Keep off the track, ladies and gentlemen!' someone was shouting. 'Please keep off the track!'

The Seven made their way through all this hurry and bustle. Anyone could come and watch the practice free, so they found a place in the last row of seats where they could see everything. The start was just below them.

'It's awfully interesting, isn't it?' said Jack. 'Each team is a different colour, so you can easily see who's who from up here.'

'There's Mike!' said Pam. 'He's all blue – his car, and his overalls, and Johnny's overalls and all the other mechanics and people belonging to his team – they're *all* sky-blue.'

'And that red team just in front of us is Curtis's,' said Peter, pointing.

'Hey, look – oh no! I don't believe it!' said Jack, suddenly sounding staggered. 'Am I dreaming, or what!'

'You're *not* dreaming if you mean you think you've seen your little sister Susie and her horrible friend Binkie!' said Peter, looking too. 'That's right – there they are, talking to Curtis's mechanic Bob!'

'Curtis himself doesn't seem to have noticed them,' said Barbara. 'To look at him, you'd think he was somewhere else entirely, not about to take part in the driving!'

'I say – Pedro Gonzalez is just going to start!' cried Pam enthusiastically.

Janet jumped up and waved to the Spanish driver to encourage him. She had liked him so much!

Pedro Gonzalez, sitting in his car and wearing his white overalls, saw her and replied with a wide smile. Janet was thrilled.

'Seven, six, five, four, three, two, one . . . ' the voice from the loudspeaker counted out the seconds.

The black and white chequered flag came down, and Pedro started. He disappeared round the first bend in a cloud of dust.

Then it was Mike Lee's turn. The young driver was very popular, and there were lots of people waving at him. Up in the seats, the Seven clapped and shouted their new friend's name, and they weren't the only ones cheering him on.

At the last moment, as the seconds were being counted out, Marianne gave Mike a kiss. Just for a moment Pam put herself in Marianne's place, and imagined what it would be like to be engaged to a racing driver who was always risking his life – she felt quite sick with fear just thinking of it! 'Oh, it must be terrible!' she whispered.

'What must be terrible?' asked Barbara, who was sitting beside her. 'What are you going on about?'

'Oh, nothing!' said Pam, embarrassed, playing with the little blue scarf she had put on when she went home at lunch-time.

Mike Lee took off at speed and disappeared round the first bend, like the drivers who had gone before him. He was followed by Angelo Giannini, the Italian, and then by a Portuguese driver, and then by a Brazilian. Jimmy Curtis was the last to drive in this first set of practice sessions.

The next two days were just the same. The drivers and their mechanics spent the mornings making adjustments and last-minute checks to the engines of their cars, and the real practice took place in the afternoons.

The Seven, particularly the four boys, watched

the drivers' performances closely. Peter had borrowed his father's large stop-watch. The children had brought their walkie-talkie radios, so that Peter and Jack could go to the finishing line and keep in touch with George and Colin, at the start.

Colin repeated the countdown into the radio set, before the flag fell. 'Seven, six, five, four, three . . .' Meanwhile, Peter would be hearing the message up in the stands at the foot of the castle. 'Two, one. He's off!'

As soon as Peter heard that, he would start the stop-watch, and about two minutes later he and Jack were hearing the car coming around the last few bends in the road. In a moment they would both see it appearing at the end of the long straight line, going at over a hundred and ten miles an hour, as Mr Lorimer had told them.

'Stop!' Jack cried at the exact moment when the car passed the finishing line down below and just in front of the two boys, and Peter would stop the watch as his friend spoke.

'Three minutes fifteen seconds!' Peter would announce. Or, 'Three minutes twenty-three seconds', or 'twenty-six seconds', or whatever the driver's time had been.

Back at the start, George and Colin carefully noted down each driver's time and the make of his vehicle. Altogether, all four boys thought this was a very good way of spending their afternoons.

The girls got a little bored with it, and wandered around the pits, looking at everything that went on backstage at a motor-racing circuit. They spent quite a lot of the third day with Marianne, Mike Lee's fiancée, who seemed very pleased to see them. 'It's so nice to have someone to talk to!' she told them. 'I hate being alone while Mike's driving – I feel quite ill with worry every time he starts, thinking he might never pass the finishing line at all.'

The girls liked Marianne very much – she tried not to show how worried she was, and was always ready to answer their questions. She even took them into those parts of the stands reserved for the race officials. While Mike was driving, they all four went into his team's pit, away from the crowd.

'Does Johnny always work with Mike?' Barbara asked their new friend.

'Yes, he does,' said Marianne. 'They've been together for more than three years now.'

'You mean Johnny goes everywhere – even when Mike's racing in America or Australia?' asked Barbara, a little surprised.

'Yes, that's right, everywhere,' Marianne told her. 'You see, the mechanic has a most important part to play. He's the one who gets the engine absolutely right and tunes it to perform as well as it possibly can. He needs to know just how the car will be driven, too, and make delicate adjustments which depend on the driver's personality. So now you can see why Mike and Johnny are an inseparable team!'

'I suppose you could say that when a driver wins

a race his mechanic has won it too, then?' said Pam.

'Indeed you could!' Marianne said. 'And Mike himself would say so!'

Just then they heard angry voices in the pit next door to them, the one belonging to the American team. Bob, the red-haired mechanic, was shouting. 'That's the key to Pit Number 8!' he yelled. 'It's mine! You stole it – you with your sneaky English ways! Give it back or you'll get your face smashed in!'

Marianne swung round.

'You're making a mistake!' Johnny protested. 'Here's your key, for goodness' sake! What a fuss to make! This pit's next to ours – the key must have been dropped just outside it.'

'That's a likely story!' snarled Bob. 'Always thinking up excuses, aren't you? Well, you just take that!'

Hearing a yell from Johnny, Marianne jumped to her feet and rushed out of the pit, with the three girls after her. They saw the two mechanics just outside the pits – they had started fighting, and Bob, who was much the bigger man, was hammering poor Johnny with his fists.

'Stop that!' said Marianne sharply, coming between them. 'Honestly, how silly! All this fuss about a dropped key!'

Looking rather taken aback and ashamed, Bob retreated. Johnny apologized again for his mistake – which the girls thought was very nice of him in the circumstances! – and walked away. As for

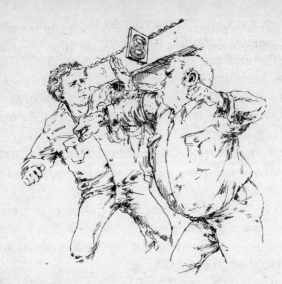

Marianne, she was still furious. She glared at Curtis, who was sitting at the back of his pit and hadn't lifted a finger to stop his mechanic attacking Johnny. He just looked back at her with a big smile.

'Thanks, lady!' he said, with a little nod of his head.

Marianne gave him a furious look too, and marched back to Mike's pit. And when the three girls started asking her more questions a little later, it was obvious that she felt so upset she didn't much want to talk, so they tactfully kept quiet.

It *had* been an upsetting little incident, too, as the boys agreed when Pam, Janet and Barbara told them about it.

But none of them could guess that something much more worrying was going to happen next day.

Chapter Five

A PUZZLE

'Hallo, that's funny!' said Colin, when the Seven arrived at the race track next morning. 'Mike's pit isn't open yet.'

'Well, he's just lying in, to make sure he's well rested. Why shouldn't he?' said Pam, springing to Mike Lee's defence.

'He's been the first to turn up over the last couple of days, though,' George pointed out. 'It's not like him to be late!'

'Especially not when it comes to crossing the finishing line!' said Janet.

The other drivers all seemed to be there with their mechanics, busy with the cars, as usual.

'Hallo, children!' called Pedro Gonzalez as they passed his pit.

'You seem pretty interested in motor racing!' added his mechanic Juan. 'We see you here every day. Thinking of going in for it yourselves?'

'No, definitely not!' said Pam with a slight shudder.

'We'll stick to watching – we're not completely – '

She stopped short, realizing all of a sudden what she had been about to say! But Pedro Gonzalez had guessed anyway.

'Completely crazy!' he finished her sentence for her. 'You're right. It takes a madman to go in for this job. You'd do better to stay in the stands, and give the winner a good round of applause, because he'll just have been risking his life!'

Then he made a funny face at the children, as if he realized he'd sounded rather serious and wanted to make light of what he'd said.

Pam managed to smile back, but she *was* feeling rather serious. For the first time, she realized that the racing drivers themselves might feel scared of the dangers they ran.

The children moved on. They saw the Italian driver, Angelo Giannini, not far off. He was a dark-haired young man who didn't smile much. You could tell he was concentrating entirely on the race and the circuit the whole time. None of the Seven had ever spoken to him, and they didn't go near his pit today either. If he wanted to be alone and concentrate before taking his car on the track, it wasn't for them to butt in.

'You know, Mike Lee *still* isn't here,' said Jack. 'And it's after ten o'clock! I don't see Johnny anywhere, either.'

'Look, there are your sister and Binkie again,' said

George. 'It looks as if Curtis's mechanic Bob has taken them under his wing.'

Looking casual about it, the Seven strolled over that way. The two little girls were deep in discussion with the American mechanic.

'Bob, how would you sabotage a bicycle chain?' Binkie was asking.

'So as to make sure it'll break after someone has started riding the bike,' Susie explained.

'Just listen to that!' said Jack furiously. 'Those two little pests and Bob make a fine team!'

'Hallo, here's the silly old Secret Seven Society!' said Binkie, when she saw the children passing.

'Are you terribly disappointed about it?' inquired Susie of the Seven in a spiteful way. 'Who'd ever have thought such a thing would happen?' The children noticed that Bob, standing behind the two girls, couldn't stop yawning, as if he were very tired.

'Oh, poor Pam!' Binkie added. 'You might as well put that blue scarf away in a drawer – it won't do anyone any good now!'

'What on earth are you two going on about?' asked Peter. 'Tell us what you mean straight out and stop dropping hints – nobody thinks they're a bit funny!'

'We do!' said Susie, with a silly grin.

'Are you or are you not going to explain?' said Jack angrily. 'You'll be sorry if you don't, I can tell you!'

'Hey, take it easy kid!' interrupted Bob, coming towards the Seven. 'Maybe you didn't hear the news, but that's not Susie and Binkie's fault!'

'What news?' asked Colin.

'Mike Lee backed out of the race. You mean you really didn't know?' said Bob, sounding as if he were rather pleased to be telling them.

'Backed out of it?' repeated Pam. She couldn't believe it!

'That's right, he backed out,' the American mechanic replied, and now he was smiling broadly. 'He's scared, see? Jimmy made the best time in practice yesterday. Mike Lee's afraid he'll lose the race and look a fool. Ha, ha, ha!' And he burst out laughing.

The Seven had had about enough of this! They

weren't going to listen to Bob and the two little pests any more — they got straight on their bicycles and rode away from Malling Castle.

Fifteen minutes later the children were rushing up the steps outside the Manor House Hotel. They ran in through the main doorway. The man at the reception desk stared at them in surprise.

'Here, where do you children think you're going?' he called indignantly.

'I expect they've come to see me,' said Mr Lorimer, who walked into the hall at that very moment. The race organizer was looking very pale. He had a yellow envelope in his hand.

'You've heard the news, I suppose?' he asked, sounding very downcast.

Peter nodded. He was looking at the piece of paper Mr Lorimer was taking out of the envelope. 'Is that from Mike?' he ventured to ask.

'That's right,' said Mr Lorimer. 'Here, you can read it. It's a telemessage.'

Peter took it, unfolded it, and read it out loud to his friends, who had gathered around him.

'I am withdrawing from the Malling Castle Motor Race, and shall probably never race again. The strain of it is just too much. Sorry if I've caused any trouble. Yours, Mike Lee.'

The Seven were struck dumb with dismay. Peter's hand shook as he gave the note back to Mr Lorimer.

'Do you realize what this means?' Mr Lorimer said, almost as if he were talking to himself. 'What a thing to do, only a couple of days before a big race! Most of the publicity for this new race depends on Mike Lee – he's the big name, and the favourite to win it! How could he do this to me?' And he furiously crumpled up the telemessage and threw it into the waste-paper basket near the reception desk, adding furiously, 'It's that girl Marianne, I'm sure it is! It's all that girl's doing!'

He was so angry that he seemed to have forgotten the children were there. They stood back to let him pass as he hurried on down the stairs and out of the hotel doors, and they saw him shake a threatening fist as he walked away.

'I don't believe it!' said Colin firmly. 'That telemessage just can't be right!'

He was pacing up and down the garden shed – not that there was very much room there for pacing up and down, but he felt so strung up that he couldn't sit still. The others were sitting on the old orange boxes they used for chairs, looking very gloomy. The news about Mike Lee had been a great blow to them.

Scamper was the only one in a good temper – and of course he didn't understand what had happened. The dog was going from one of the children to another, hoping for a game, but no one was in the mood for playing with him. Poor Scamper.

'What we've got to do is go and see Mike,' said Peter, making up his mind to a plan of action. 'If we hear it from his own lips, then we'll just *have* to believe he's backing out of the race! But until then – well, there could be some mistake.'

'How can we go and see him?' said Barbara. 'He isn't in this part of the country any more, is he? I mean, if he sent a telemessage, that means he's somewhere quite a long way off.'

'We can find out his home telephone number from Mr Lorimer and ring him up,' said Peter sensibly.

'Do you think he'll be *at* his home, though?' said George.

Peter thought about this. 'You've got a point,' he agreed. 'He won't want to face the public and the Press just yet – backing out of a big race like this looks such a cowardly thing for a racing driver to do!'

'He didn't back out of it!' Colin insisted, raising his voice. 'I tell you he didn't! Why, only yesterday he was telling us that racing was his whole life! And you don't change your mind overnight about a thing like that, do you? Just think how hard he's had to work to get up into the top class of racing drivers! Imagine what will-power it took! Do you honestly think he's going to drop his career now, after all the effort he's put into it? I mean, what else does life hold for him? Well, I ask you!'

'Marianne, since you're asking us!' said Pam, interrupting Colin's long speech. And then, in a quiet

50

voice, she explained what she meant. 'Marianne's his fiancée. He loves her. Surely he'd think more of her than winning all the motor races in the world!'

This idea simply took Colin's breath away. He sat down rather suddenly! When he could manage to speak again, he said, 'Well, if we're going to look at it in *that* sort of way . . .'

But he couldn't bring himself to finish his sentence. It was too shocking to think that Pam's idea might be correct!

What was more, Pam was following it up. 'Have you thought what it's like for a racing-driver's wife?' she went on. 'All that anxiety the whole time! At the start of every race Marianne's wondering if she'll see Mike alive again. Or perhaps if she does, if he'll be injured and in pain – he might even be paralysed and unable to walk any more!'

There was dead silence in the garden shed as everyone thought about these dreadful possibilities. Even Scamper kept still, as if in sympathy.

'Well, I can easily see Mike thinking he has no right to inflict all that on his fiancée,' Pam finished. She had brought tears to her own eyes!

But Colin wasn't having any of this. He jumped up again, protesting, 'That sounds very sad and so on – but *I* think you've been reading too many soppy stories!'

Pam uttered an indignant exclamation.

'Mind, I don't say Marianne and Mike aren't very

fond of each other,' Colin went on, speaking mainly to Pam. 'But how do you explain the fact that he was determined to do his best to win the Malling Castle Motor Race when we talked to him yesterday – and today he's just disappeared? What's love got to do with that? You don't back out of a motor race during practice, once you've entered for it. It just doesn't make sense!'

'Hear, hear!' agreed George. 'Especially since Marianne was there all day yesterday too, and she didn't seem upset or anything.'

'She did tell Pam and Barbara and me that she was always worrying about Mike,' Janet told them.

'Well, all right, but what does that prove?' said Colin. 'It's natural for her to worry, isn't it? But Marianne's a good sort – she doesn't go making a big fuss about it when she knows that might upset Mike! I tell you, there's something very puzzling about all this. 'It doesn't seem like Mike at all.'

'I quite agree,' said Peter, who had been keeping fairly quiet but thinking hard. 'It *is* a puzzle.'

'And one we could investigate,' said Jack. 'Think of all the puzzles we've solved before – why not this one? We could start by trying to find out more of the facts. We don't know just when he left, or how.'

'Johnny may be able to tell us,' suggested Barbara.

'And I wouldn't be surprised if Mr Lorimer knows more than he's letting on,' said Janet.

The discussion went on a good deal longer, and

the Seven drew up a plan of action. By the time their meeting was over, Colin was seething with impatience. 'Come on!' he told the others. 'We've already wasted two whole hours. Let's get moving!'

He flung open the door of the garden shed.

'Come on, Scamper!' Peter told the spaniel. 'You can come with us today – there aren't any racing cars where we're going now!'

The Seven picked up their bicycles, which they had left leaning against the garden fence. Nobody had tried tying them together this afternoon!

'I bet those two little pests are still plotting horrible

things with Bob!' thought Jack, feeling cross, as he usually did when he thought of Susie's mean tricks.

He didn't know how right he was!

Chapter Six

AT THE HOTEL

The man at the reception desk of the Manor House Hotel frowned and opened his mouth to protest when he saw the children coming in again. But Peter gave him a polite smile, and said, 'Excuse me – we're Mr Lorimer's friends! Don't you remember us from this morning? We – er – some of us have to go and see somebody upstairs. We won't be long.'

The man nodded in a rather grudging way, and let them go past the desk.

'Right, girls!' Peter said in a low voice. 'You see about the waste-paper basket. Colin and Jack, you wander about the hotel trying to look inconspicuous, and find out what you can. Jack and I are going to look for Johnny.'

They separated into three groups, and Peter and Jack went over to the lift. Luckily they knew where Johnny's room was – Number 35, on the third floor, because Mike had insisted on having his mechanic staying in the same hotel. The two boys went up in the lift and then down the long corridor, which had such thick red carpet that you couldn't hear your own footsteps on it.

'Here we are – Room 35,' said Peter. He knocked on the door.

Three seconds – ten seconds – twenty seconds passed, and there was no reply. Peter knocked again.

'Who's that?' Johnny asked, sounding rather far away.

'It's us – the Secret Seven. Well, Jack and Peter, anyway,' said Jack, putting his mouth close to the door.

'I don't want to be disturbed,' said Johnny. His voice sounded just as faint as before.

'Honestly, we'll only be a minute!' Peter told him.

'No, sorry, I'm in bed,' said the mechanic.

'But it's about Mike,' Jack went on. 'We'd like to know what – '

'I don't know much myself!' said Johnny, interrupting him. 'Just leave me in peace, will you?'

'Please let us talk to you!' Peter said.

'Only for a minute!' Jack repeated.

But it was no use. Johnny wouldn't say anything. They tried pleading with him a little longer, and then gave it up.

When they came down the big flight of stairs, they found George and Colin on the first-floor balcony.

'We've drawn a blank,' Peter admitted. It wasn't something he liked to confess.

'Johnny just won't let us into his room,' said Jack. 'Obviously he's terribly upset. I wonder if he does know anything?'

'Well, we do,' said Colin, but he didn't sound very happy about it.

'What?' asked Peter. 'And how did you find out?'

'From the chamber-maid,' said George. 'The one who was on duty yesterday evening. She saw it all.'

'That's right – Mike and Marianne were having a loud, angry argument,' Colin went on. 'That's what the chamber-maid told us. It went on for at least a quarter of an hour, and then they hurried out of the hotel.'

'So it looks as if Pam's theory was right,' said Jack. 'Marianne made Mike choose between her and his life as a racing driver.'

'And Mike gave in to her!' said Peter.

'I must say, I feel really disappointed in him,' said Colin.

Sadly, the boys went down the stairs to the hotel hall – where a surprising sight met their eyes and took their minds off the unsatisfactory result of their inquiries. Scamper, who was usually such a good, well-behaved dog, was rolling on the floor with his paws in the air, wagging his tail, turning round and round, and generally making a nuisance of himself! Pam, Barbara and Janet were trying to calm him down, but it was no good. The way he was carrying on, he was bound to knock something over before

long, and sure enough, he did! The waste-paper basket, which was standing just in front of the reception
desk fell over, scattering all its contents.

The boys hurried down the last few stairs, the
man at the desk came round to pick things up, the
girls were exclaiming and retrieving the waste paper
and trying to get Scamper under control.

'For goodness' sake, take that dog out of here!'
said the man at the reception desk, exasperated.
'This is a hotel, you know, not a menagerie!'

'Oh, I'm awfully sorry!' said Janet.

'He's never like this usually,' added Barbara. 'I've never known him do such a thing before.'

'There – we've tidied everything up!' said Pam, who had been working busily away. 'All the waste paper's back in the basket now. We really are most *terribly* sorry!'

Peter had grabbed hold of Scamper and was dragging him out of the door. The other children followed as fast as they could – and the man at the reception desk heaved a sigh of relief as they left.

'Got it!' said Pam at the foot of the steps leading up to the hotel doors. And she showed the others a little ball of crumpled paper – the telemessage!

'Well done!' said Colin. 'That was jolly clever of you, Pam!'

'It's Scamper who did the clever bit,' said Pam. 'If he hadn't sensed what was wanted and played up like that, we'd never have got hold of it.'

'The man at the desk was watching everything we did,' Barbara went on. 'There just wasn't any way at all to get at the waste-paper basket.'

'Let's have a look!' said Peter, taking the telemessage. He flattened the paper quickly against his leg with the palm of his hand, and read out the words he had seen once before.

'I am withdrawing from the Malling Castle Motor Race, and shall probably never race again. The strain of it is just too much. Sorry if I've caused any trouble. Yours, Mike Lee.'

'We knew that already!' said Jack impatiently. 'Where was it sent from?'

'Malling Post Office, at nine-fifteen today!' said Peter.

'Then he must have sent it just after leaving the hotel this morning,' said Barbara. 'I suppose they delivered it today because it was for a local address.'

'That's about it – Mike had his argument with Marianne yesterday evening, thought about it all night, and took his decision this morning,' said Colin.

'What argument with Marianne?' asked Pam. 'What are you talking about?'

'The chamber-maid told us they had an argument – that's how we know,' George told her.

'I see,' said Pam. She didn't sound pleased – it was hard for her to believe that Mike and Marianne could quarrel. They'd seemed such a happy, easy-going couple, and were both so friendly to the children.

Suddenly Scamper started to growl. Peter, who had him on his lead, found it quite hard to hold him back.

'A cat – that's all we needed!' said Janet, pointing to a little tabby cat which was sitting not far away.

The spaniel tugged frantically at his lead, barking at the cat.

'Calm down, Scamper!' Peter told him. 'Good dog – calm down!'

'Did you girls find out anything else that might be useful while we were up on the top floors?' Colin asked.

'Not really,' said Pam. 'Oh, wait a minute, though!' she suddenly remembered. 'Mr Lorimer hurried by, and we had a quick word with him – he told us he'd phoned all the numbers where he thought he might be able to get hold of Mike.'

'What happened?' asked Jack.

'Nothing,' said Barbara. 'I mean, either there wasn't any answer, or the people at the other end of the line hadn't seen Mike or heard from him.'

'That's odd,' muttered Colin. 'And I still think there's something peculiar about the telemessage. I can't make anything much of the quarrel Mike and Marianne had, either.'

But he got no further with his thinking aloud, because Scamper, who had been tugging at his lead all this time, suddenly managed to break free of Peter's grip and chase off after the cat.

'Scamper! Scamper! Come back this minute!' Peter shouted after him. He ran after the dog, with the others chasing close behind.

Luckily the chase didn't last long. The cat took refuge in the Manor House Hotel's car park – it had been built underground, so as not to spoil the countryside views from the hotel windows. Scamper lost his prey in the dim light, among all the cars, and stopped running. Jack found him lying under-

neath a car, feeling very ashamed of himself for letting the cat escape, and obviously knowing he was a bad dog and expecting punishment!

Sure enough, the children *did* scold Scamper, who was usually so well-behaved. Then, suddenly, Peter let out a cry of surprise.

'Look – see that at the back of the garage?' he asked the others, pointing.

'Goodness, yes – it's Mike's own car, no doubt about it!' said Colin. He was delighted. 'So I was right, and he hasn't left these parts after all!'

All the Secret Seven went over to look at the car. Yes, it really was Mike Lee's car, sky-blue like his racing outfits, and with a moulded black plastic driving seat. Pam noticed a little round frame containing a photograph of Marianne set into the dashboard. Marianne was smiling in a very attractive way in the picture. 'I'm *sure* they didn't have any quarrel! It's just not true!' she said firmly.

'Well, if he hasn't left these parts, he's in hiding,' said Jack, following up the train of thought that their discovery suggested.

'But he's got no reason to hide!' objected Barbara. 'You don't mean to say you think he's afraid of Jimmy Curtis, do you – on or off the race track?'

'No, he isn't hiding,' said Colin. 'I tell you what the answer is – he's *been hidden*!'

Chapter Seven

MORE AND MORE MYSTERIOUS!

'Mike's been hidden?' said Janet, puzzled. 'Whatever do you mean?'

'I mean he's been kidnapped, that's what!' said Colin.

'Been reading a few too many exciting spy stories, have you, Colin?' asked Peter kindly, shaking his head.

'I don't see why anyone should have kidnapped Mike, myself,' said George, agreeing with Peter. 'If you're thinking some rival driver came along and kidnapped him out of spite, Colin – well, that sort of thing's usually settled in a straightforward way on the race track!'

'There might be some other reason we don't know,' said Colin, sticking to his guns. 'Like – well, for instance, like money!'

'Mike's still very young,' Barbara pointed out. 'He hasn't got years and years of a successful career behind him. He can't be a millionaire yet.'

'Or perhaps . . . ' Jack began.

'Yes? Perhaps what?' asked Peter.

'Perhaps Marianne's broken off the engagement, and he wasn't expecting it, and it was such a terrible shock he backed out of the race in his despair!'

'That's a bit far-fetched, isn't it?' said Colin sarcastically.

'Well, we must find out more,' said Peter. 'I'm off to Malling to see if the postmistress there can tell us anything. You come with me, Jack. I want the girls to go back into the hotel and have another go at Johnny – he may be a bit more polite and feel like opening his door today! I suggest Colin and George go off to the circuit and wander around, keeping their ears and eyes well open. We'll meet in the garden shed at six o'clock.'

The Seven emerged from the hotel car park and set off in different directions. Peter had decided that Scamper was to go with himself and Jack. A nice long run might calm the spaniel down a bit!

It was a busy afternoon for all the children. They did their best to carry out their missions. The village church was just striking six as Pam, Barbara and Janet joined the boys in the shed.

'Golly, I'm worn out!' sighed Janet, sitting down on an orange box.

'Johnny wouldn't let us talk to him,' Barbara told the boys. 'He wouldn't even open the door! All he'd tell us, from the other side of it, was that if Mike had left his car here that meant he'd travelled by train – and that was all we could get out of him!'

'So then we gave up and went to a tea-shop,' said Pam, 'and I had three cream buns.'

At these interesting words Scamper raised his head and licked his chops hopefully.

'And I had two chocolate eclairs,' added Janet.

'Oh, marvellous! What a strenuous way to go making inquiries!' said Peter sarcastically. 'You're great detectives, you really are!'

'Well, we couldn't help it if Johnny wouldn't come out of his room or let us into it, could we?' said Barbara indignantly.

'I just hope George and Colin have found out a bit more, that's all,' said Peter, turning to the two boys. 'How did you get on?'

'Not too well, I'm afraid,' said George. 'They're still having practice sessions on the circuit – the drivers' times are getting better and better as they come to know the track.'

'Apart from that, well, Jimmy Curtis is definitely the favourite now Mike's out of the race. Everyone expects him to win. And that's about all,' said Colin. 'We're really not much further on than we were this morning!'

'Oh, and we met Susie and Binkie again,' George remembered. 'They're thick as thieves with Bob, that American mechanic. When we arrived they were telling him about good places to visit in this part of the country. Bob's interested in old buildings, apparently.'

'Never mind Bob's hobbies! They're nothing to do with us,' said Peter. He didn't like the fat, red-haired man at all.

'Well, Peter and I *did* discover something!' said Jack. Ever since the meeting began, he'd been looking forward to this moment.

'Yes – we found out that it wasn't Mike who sent Mr Lorimer that telemessage!' Peter told the rest of the Seven.

'What?' cried Pam, jumping up.

'At first the postmistress wouldn't tell us anything. She kept saying it would be very unprofessional of her. Scamper was starting to growl and show his teeth – I had to keep a careful eye on him,' said Peter.

'Then I actually showed her the telemessage,' Jack went on. 'I asked if the man who sent it had been young, about twenty years old, and dark-haired, and so on.'

'And she immediately said no!' Peter went on. 'No, it wasn't a man of twenty, and he wasn't dark – she was quite sure of that. But she refused to tell us any more.'

'I thought that telemessage was fishy all along,' said Colin.

'So it looks as if Mike really *has* been kidnapped,' said George.

'How awful – poor Mike!' said Barbara. 'The trouble

is, even knowing that doesn't get us very far! We don't know who sent the fake telemessage, and we haven't the faintest idea where Mike may be held prisoner.'

'We'd better go to the police, hadn't we?' suggested Janet.

'No, certainly not!' Barbara told her. 'That would be risky – while Mike's still in the kidnappers' hands, there could be reprisals.'

'Re-whats?' said Colin, who didn't know the word.

'Well, call it vengeance if you'd rather,' said Peter. 'Suppose the kidnapper or kidnappers get to know the police are after them and they feel they're being tracked down, they might hurt Mike, or even threaten to kill him!'

The Seven shivered with horror. Pam tightened the knot of the little blue scarf she was still wearing round her neck. She thought of Marianne and her lovely smile in the photograph on the dashboard of Mike's car. No, of course it wouldn't do to tell the police!

The Seven would have to tread very, very carefully and think what they were doing – it was possible that a man's life was in their hands, and they all felt that man was a personal friend of theirs.

Next morning the girls went to the hotel and knocked at Johnny's door. 'It's us again – Pam and Janet and me!' Barbara called through it. 'Do open your door, Johnny. This is very, very important!'

Johnny didn't budge.

'Listen, Mike's life could depend on it!' Janet begged him.

'He's been kidnapped!' Pam said desperately.

At these words the miracle finally happened! The key turned in the lock of the door, and Johnny appeared. 'Come in,' he told the three girls.

He offered them the chairs that stood in one corner of the room and sat down on the edge of his bed opposite them. He looked pale and drawn, and obviously hadn't slept much that night, if at all.

'What's all this about? Mike can't possibly have been kidnapped!' he said in a tired voice. 'Have you tried ringing his home telephone number?'

'He isn't there, honestly,' Janet assured the mechanic. 'Mr Lorimer tried phoning everywhere he could possibly be yesterday, but he had no luck at all.'

'What about Marianne?' asked Johnny. 'Did he call Marianne?'

'I don't think so,' Pam admitted. 'He mentioned a whole list of people and places he'd tried, but I don't think Marianne was among them.'

'Come to think of it, he probably hasn't got her number,' said Johnny suddenly. 'Mr Lorimer's the race organizer – he only knows Marianne through Mike, not personally.'

'Why don't we ring her now?' suggested Barbara.

Johnny willingly agreed to that, and dialled Marianne's number at once. 'Hallo, Marianne – Johnny here!' he said.

'Oh, my goodness – I do hope nothing's happened to Mike!' said Marianne at the other end of the line at once, sounding very worried.

'No, no, Mike's fine!' the mechanic assured her.

'I suppose he asked you to ring me, did he?'

'Er . . . yes,' Johnny said.

'Listen, would you tell him I see now I was quite wrong?' Marianne asked. 'I went off in a temper. We were quarrelling all the way to the station, and we parted on the platform before we'd made things up.'

'Well, these things happen, and then they – they sort of blow over,' said Johnny, very embarrassed.

'Can I speak to him?' she asked hopefully.

'No, I'm afraid not – he's on the track at the moment.'

'Oh dear!' Marianne sighed. 'Then would you tell him I'm going to get the very next train, and I'll be with him this evening?'

'Yes . . . yes, of course. He'll be delighted,' said Johnny. 'Well – see you soon, Marianne.' And he put the receiver down, looking shattered.

Pam was crying.

'I'm afraid I just didn't have the courage to tell her the truth,' said the mechanic. 'But I'll have to let her know this evening, of course.'

'Maybe we'll have found him by then!' said Barbara hopefully.

'Don't you think maybe he just went off to be on his own and think, after he had that quarrel with Marianne?' suggested Janet. The three girls had been able to catch almost every word Marianne said over the telephone.

'No,' said Pam, shaking her head. 'Remember – we know the telemessage Mr Lorimer got this morning wasn't really sent by Mike at all.'

Then Barbara and Janet told Johnny the whole story – and he had to admit that they must be right.

'I can't get over it!' he said, bewildered. The news was obviously a great blow to him. 'Who could have done such a terrible thing?'

'We hoped *you'd* have some idea – that's why we

came to see you!' said Barbara, very disappointed to find that Johnny seemed just as puzzled as they were.

Johnny scratched his head and looked at the ceiling. 'It's no good, however hard I think I can't come up with anything – unless of course . . . no, that really couldn't be it!'

'Oh, Johnny!' the girls all begged him. 'Please, *please* do tell us what you've thought of!'

Chapter Eight

GETTING SOMEWHERE AT LAST

The four boys were seeing what they could find out at the race track. They kept hard at work amidst the noise of engines and voices, looking for anyone who might be able to help them.

There must be *someone* in the crowd thronging round the racing cars who knew something – someone who could give them a clue. Even if it was only a tiny one, it might start them on the right line of inquiry.

George and Colin had made their way towards Angelo Giannini, the Italian driver. Giannini was just getting ready to go on the track. His mechanic closed the heavy bonnet of the car and jerked his thumb to tell the driver that everything was in order.

Angelo Giannini adjusted the strap of his helmet. The boys boldly marched up and addressed him. 'I say, Mr Giannini,' said George, 'now that Mike Lee is out of the race, do you think the result is as important as before?'

'Yes, and why did he back out? Do you have any ideas about *that*?' Colin added, without giving the Italian time to answer the first question.

'No, I no got no idea,' was all the Italian driver said, and he nervously touched a little holy picture which the two boys saw on the dashboard of his racing car.

The chequered flag went down and the engine of Giannini's car roared. He shot away without another word to the two boys, who were left no wiser than before.

'I've a feeling he does know something,' said George, as the racing car disappeared around the first bend. 'Did you see the way he touched his picture, as if for luck?'

'Just superstition,' said Colin. 'Mike told us that all racing drivers are very superstitious, and I bet Giannini feels Mike dropping out like that is a bad omen.'

'You may be right,' sighed George. He was disappointed that they hadn't managed to get anything more out of the Italian driver.

Not far off, in the Spanish driver's pit, Peter and Jack were talking to Pedro Gonzalez, who was in his spotless white overalls as usual.

'Do you really think Mike backed out of his own free will?' Peter was asking him.

'You see, only the day before he was telling us about all his plans, and the contracts he was signing,'

Jack added. 'He told us how he loved motor racing, and all the competition! So why should he suddenly drop out of the race and say he's giving up the sport altogether?'

'I don't know – I really don't know!' said Gonzalez, looking as puzzled as the boys were themselves. 'Mike was at the start of a wonderful career – he'd risen to the top really fast, and looked like staying there, and everyone in the sport liked him. Of course he made mistakes at first, just like all of us, but – '

'What sort of mistakes?' asked Peter curiously, interrupting him.

'Well, once or twice he got in another driver's way while he was racing,' Gonzalez explained. 'But that can happen to the greatest champions, and it was obvious Mike did it because he was inexperienced at the time, not out of spite. He was very young, you know, when he started racing.'

'Time to go, Pedro!' shouted Juan, coming into the pit quite out of breath. 'You start in a minute! Come along – the engine's turning over!'

'Sorry, boys!' said the Spanish driver, with a smile. He picked up his helmet and strode out. At that very moment a voice over the loudspeakers called for him to come to the start. Peter and Jack left the pit too, and joined George and Colin again. The four boys went over to the American's pit together.

'And of course those two little pests have to be

there!' groaned Colin, spotting Susie and Binkie chatting to Bob the mechanic again.

'What on earth can they be talking about?' Jack wondered. 'Susie's never shown the slightest interest in cars of any kind before.'

The boys went closer. Bob was tuning Jimmy Curtis's engine, while the two little girls leaned over to watch him at work. They didn't see the boys coming.

'I say – see that?' Colin asked his friends suddenly, in a low voice, when they were closer to the pit. 'Bob's boots! Do look at his boots!'

'Covered with mud!' whispered Peter.

'And it hasn't been raining,' said George in the same low tones. 'Where can he have been?'

Even if the others had known the answer, they

wouldn't have had time to tell him, because at that moment Binkie noticed them.

'Spying on us again!' she said, furiously.

Susie was cross too. She went over to her brother Jack and shook a black, oily finger at him. 'You just leave us alone, you and your horrible friends, or I'll put oil all over your faces!' she threatened, making a face at him.

'Don't you dare, or I'll strangle you!' said Jack, just as cross as she was!

Jimmy Curtis appeared just then, and couldn't help grinning as he saw the brother and sister quarrelling. However, his arrival put an end to the argument – Susie lowered her oily finger, and Jack turned and marched away.

The Seven met in the garden shed at two o'clock that afternoon. Scamper was there too, and seemed to be listening to everything the children said with great interest.

The girls spoke up first, and told the story of how they had at last been able to talk to Johnny properly. They described his telephone call to Marianne, and warned the boys that she was coming back herself that evening. The boys reported on their conversations with the other racing drivers – and Jack mentioned his argument with Susie and Binkie!

'Jimmy Curtis arrived just in time – for them!' he said. 'I'd have turned them into sausage-meat given another minute!'

Everybody laughed.

'But none of this gets us much closer to finding Mike!' said George, in a firm tone which reminded them all that the situation was really serious.

'Johnny did have an idea who might have done it, but he made us promise not to say anything,' said Barbara hesitantly. 'Besides, he's almost certain he's wrong.'

'And he's afraid it would make trouble,' added Janet.

'What on earth do you mean? What sort of trouble?' said Colin crossly. 'Why all this caution? Don't be so silly! Don't you realize Mike's life may be at stake?'

'Who *does* Johnny suspect?' Peter asked the three girls sternly. 'Come on, you *have* to tell us.'

'He made us promise not to tell!' wailed poor Barbara.

'All right, then,' said Colin, looking quite white with anger. 'But if anything happens to Mike, just remember it'll be on your consciences!'

'It's Bob!' Pam blurted out.

'Bob!' said George, echoing her. 'Well, I know he's not very nice, but that doesn't mean he's a kidnapper!'

'And why would he want to kidnap Mike Lee?' asked Jack. 'I honestly can't see any sense in it.'

'It's obvious that Johnny detests Bob and Bob hates Johnny – we can see that for ourselves,' said

Peter. 'But what would Bob have against Mike? I call that a pretty nonsensical idea!'

'All the same, Bob *is* a rather strange sort of person,' said Colin thoughtfully, frowning. 'Remember the first day of practice, and how he sent us off when we passed the American pit?'

'And he had that fight over nothing with Johnny next day,' Janet reminded the others. 'Marianne had to separate them!'

'And he's been yawning like anything for the last two days, as if he weren't getting enough sleep,' Colin went on. 'He was at it again this morning – I saw him yawning away over the engine of Curtis's car.'

'And what about those muddy boots of his?' said Jack. 'Where's he been in *them*?'

'Going for walks and exploring the country, I suppose,' said Barbara. 'He's interested in old buildings – or so George told us yesterday.'

'That's right,' George said. 'Susie and Binkie were giving him all sorts of information about old buildings locally – walls and churches and ruins and things.'

'You mean he's going about the place sight-seeing by night?' Colin asked. 'Now that really *is* strange!'

'By night?' said Barbara, surprised.

'He was half asleep, working on the engine of Curtis's car this morning,' said Colin. 'I'll bet you anything he can hardly have had a proper night's sleep this week!'

'And it was at night that Mike disappeared, as far as we can make out!' Pam cried suddenly.

There was a long silence, as all the Seven realized that Bob really could have been the kidnapper!

Chapter Nine

SEARCHING FOR MIKE

The Seven went into action at once. In less time
than it takes to tell, they had jumped on their bicycles
and were cycling all round the local roads.

Pam and Janet went to look at a deserted farm-
house in the middle of the cornfields – it was only
a shell of a building now, and people avoided it
because it was said to be haunted. There were no
signs of any ghosts – but when they pushed open
the old door which, surprisingly, was still in place,
and went into a large room without any roof, they
disturbed a whole family of owls. Pam was so scared
that she screeched like an owl herself, but Janet,
who didn't mind birds or any other living creatures,
searched the whole place carefully. However, she
found no trace at all of Mike Lee.

Barbara and George went off to an old railway
tunnel on a disused part of the line. It had collapsed
over fifty years ago, but you could still go a little
way along it, and its mouth was half-hidden by bram-

bles, so the children thought it was a possible place to hide a kidnap victim. They went along it as far as they could, but here again they found no trace of any human being, and they crawled back along the part of the tunnel that was still open and back into the daylight.

Peter took Scamper and climbed up to Torling Castle – not a proper castle like Malling, where the racing circuit had been constructed, only a ruined one. The Seven had had adventures at Torling Castle before. A great round tower rose from the ruins, with no way to get into it at ground level, so Peter decided

to climb the fifteen metres or so to the nearest loophole. He was able to get up quite easily with the help of the ivy that grew all over the tower. Its thick, gnarled stems had rooted themselves between the old stones, and gave him good hand-holds. Scamper watched him climb, looking as if he wished he could go up too. With his tail beating the ground, the spaniel gave a little yelp now and then as if he was afraid Peter might fall.

But he didn't. He reached the loophole, got his head through it, and then shouted at the top of his voice, 'Mike! Mike! This is Peter – Peter from the Secret Seven, you remember? Are you anywhere in there, Mike?'

His voice echoed and re-echoed inside the tower, and then died away in a deep silence.

The tower was pitch black inside, and Peter couldn't see a thing. He shivered!

'Mike! Mike!' he shouted again, but without much hope of a reply. And indeed the echo was the only reply he got. Peter had to admit to himself that the tower was empty.

As for Jack and Colin, they had left their bicycles by a small bridge overgrown with brambles, and then walked up the dry bed of what had once been a branch of the river. After they had gone a little way they came to an old, disused water-mill. The building was almost entirely hidden under tangled vegetation – only its roof showed, and that had been

broken in places by falling branches. The two boys
knew this place well. They scrambled under the old
wooden mill-wheel and found a little door hidden
behind a thicket of stinging nettles, leading into the
mill itself.

They went down a dark, damp corridor – and
when they emerged into the old living-room of the
mill they were surprised and delighted to hear someone speak their names. 'Jack! Colin! I'm over here!'

It was Mike!

They soon spotted him at the back of the room,
sitting in front of the empty fireplace. He was busy
eating a sandwich.

'You seem to be doing all right!' said Colin, looking at it.

'Depends what you mean!' said the young racing driver, showing them his ankle – it had a chain round it, and the chain was fastened to a ring in the wall. 'If I ever get my hands on that man Bob . . . ' he said grimly.

'So it *was* Bob!' said Jack. 'We'd begun to suspect him!'

'Well, we'll soon get you out of here,' Colin told Mike. 'And won't Bob look surprised when he sees you arrive at the track tomorrow!'

'I wish you *could* get me out of here – but how?' said Mike, tugging at the chain to show Jack and Colin how solid it was.

'I think I'd better go back to the village,' said Jack. 'I'll let the others know and collect some tools. And then we'll all come and set you free.'

'I'll stay with Mike,' Colin decided.

Wasting no more time, Jack set off again. He went down the damp little corridor, under the worm-eaten wooden mill-wheel, along the dry bed of the river, and picked up his bike at the bridge. While he was pedalling home as fast as he could go, Mike and Colin sat in the dim light of the mill, and Mike told Colin what had happened.

'I took Marianne to the station on Thursday evening,' he said. 'We went on foot – we felt we needed a walk, we'd had a bit of a quarrel. I left her on the platform as her train was coming in, and went back to the hotel. It wasn't very late, so I thought I'd like a stroll in the countryside – I got more of a stroll than I bargained for! I went the couple of miles into your village, and that's where Bob jumped me, in a dark little lane by the church. He must have been following me, but I never heard him coming – I just felt something hit me on the back of the head, right above the nape of my neck.'

Colin felt Mike's skull. Yes, sure enough, there was a huge bump on his head under his hair.

'When I came round I was somewhere in the woods, tied to a tree,' Mike went on. 'The sun rose, and I spent all day there unable to move. I called and called, but it was pretty obvious that my attacker would have left me somewhere nobody would hear me. I didn't yet know who the attacker was, either, not till evening when Bob turned up. He'd come to take me to this mill, where he chained me up to that ring in the wall, left me with a bag of food, and then went off again, saying he'd be back and let me go on the evening after the race.'

'Why didn't you escape on the way to the mill?' Colin wondered. 'Bob's fat and heavy – I'm sure you could easily have got away from him!'

'Yes, but he had a gun!' said Mike. 'He told me he'd shoot if I made the slightest move to run for it – and I didn't feel like taking any chances on that!'

'He must be crazy!' said Colin. 'That's what he

is, crazy! How could he hope to get away with this? He knows you know him, and once you're free you'll go to the police.'

'What he most wanted, he said, was to keep me from driving in the race, and afterwards – well, he told me he'd have his revenge on Marianne if I went to the police. I'm sure that was only blustering, though. The main idea was to keep me from taking part in the race.'

'But why?' asked Colin. 'What's he got to lose if you win it?'

'Oh, a great deal,' said Mike. 'A mechanic has the same hopes and fears as a driver, you know, and his responsibility for winning or losing a race is almost as great as the driver's too. Success or defeat is largely due to him.'

'Yes, I see,' said Colin. 'But if all mechanics tried this sort of thing on the drivers of rival teams, there wouldn't be many drivers at the start of a race at all!'

'Quite true,' said Mike. 'But Bob has a grudge against me anyway. When I was starting in my career, I did some clumsy things at times. One day, racing on a circular track, I found myself driving close to Curtis, our wheels very near each other. Curtis was actually in the lead, because I was two laps behind. I tried to overtake, but I was too close, and I just caught him. He had to brake to avoid a bad crash, and he went off the track and into the straw. He lost that race, and it was my fault. Bob felt it badly – he didn't get the bonus he could have expected if Curtis won. He's hated me ever since, and worse than ever since last year when I won the championship.'

Mike was obviously very upset by the whole thing.

'What about Jimmy Curtis?' Colin ventured to ask. 'Where does he come into this?'

'Oh, he doesn't, I'm sure of that,' said Mike. 'I've nothing against him at all.'

Then he fell silent, and Colin realized it would be

tactless to ask any more questions. They stayed there in silence for over half an hour before they suddenly heard voices calling, and a familiar bark. A few moments later the whole Secret Seven came into the mill, with the faithful Scamper.

Peter was carrying his father's tool-bag, and found a suitable metal saw. Jack wedged part of the chain firmly between two large stones, while George and Colin held this makeshift work-bench steady. Taking turns, the boys began to saw at a link in the chain.

While they worked away, the girls gave Mike a drink. He hadn't had anything for two days – Bob had thought of sandwiches, but he had completely forgotten that his prisoner might get thirsty, as indeed Mike did. He was grateful to the girls for bringing a thermos flask of tea with them.

Slowly but surely the saw bit into the chain. A tiny pinch of iron filings fell every time it passed back or forth. They had to stop sawing several times and pour water on the chain to cool the metal. Mike encouraged them. He was obviously very worried, and kept looking at his watch, afraid Bob might turn up at any moment.

At last the link gave way! Using hammers and pincers, the boys managed to get the chain apart – and Mike was free.

'And tomorrow you'll win the race!' cried Pam.

'And pay Bob back!' said Jack happily.

'The first thing to do is get away from this place,'

said Mike. 'I wouldn't want to meet him here – remember that gun of his!'

'Won't he be surprised to see nothing but the end of a chain!' said Janet, laughing.

Night was falling as they came out of the mill. They groped their way along the dry river-bed and got back to the bicycles they had left on the bridge. Mike borrowed Peter's bike and took Janet, the smallest of the Seven, on the carrier, so that they could all ride.

They cycled back to the village, avoiding the main road. On their way, they decided that it was too risky for Mike to go back to the Manor House Hotel, so he would spend the night with Peter and Janet's parents. Pam would go to the station with Barbara to meet Marianne, and tell her the whole story, and one of them would ask Marianne back to her house to spend the night there. Meanwhile Jack, George and Colin would go and find Mr Lorimer at the Manor House Hotel and tell him Mike was back.

Of course Peter and Janet's parents were very pleased to have Mike to stay – and next day, the day of the race, to the amazement of everyone present, Mike Lee, world champion driver, appeared at the race track!

Chapter Ten

THE RACE BEGINS

Johnny was delighted – he couldn't stop whistling happily. In his pleasure, he had polished Mike's racing car all over, so that it shone in the sunlight!

The spectators were gradually filling the stands. There were several rows of seats all along the track, behind the bales of straw. Of course the Seven were there too, on guard outside Mike's pit.

At twenty past two Jimmy Curtis arrived, looking as imperturbable as ever. The sinister figure of Bob followed him. Curtis went into his pit without so much as a glance at Mike – but Bob gave him a very black look. Susie and Binkie, the two little pests, were there too, passing silly remarks and making stupid jokes.

'Ha, ha, ha, hee, hee, hee! Jimmy will win and not Mike Lee!' sang Susie, to the tune of 'Little Brown Jug'. She was very proud of her song.

Jack was going to smack his little sister, but Peter stopped him. 'Take no notice!' he said firmly. 'Our

difference of opinion will be settled on the track, fair and square!'

The first cars were already being rolled out towards the start. The loudspeakers had stopped broadcasting music and were announcing the order in which the drivers would race. It was decided by the times they had recorded in the practice sessions. Curtis, who had the best score, would be the last to set off. Of course Mike couldn't benefit at all by this arrangement, because he had missed two whole days of training. He was thirty-second out of the forty-nine competitors.

There was a very large crowd – so big that after a while the attendants wouldn't let any more people into the stands in case they collapsed. There had never been such excitement in this usually quiet part of the country before!

It was as good as a fun-fair, and in fact there were plenty of stalls, either selling things to eat and drink, or souvenirs. The race track was bright with balloons, bunting and flags.

While the crowd waited for the first car to start, the loudspeaker went on with the announcements. When the voice mentioned that Mike Lee was taking part, there was a roar of applause all the way from the start to the finishing line. Everyone was delighted to see the champion here.

At this moment Marianne turned up to wish her fiancée good luck. She was looking very tense, and wore a pretty dress. Pam watched, drinking in the scene, as the engaged couple talked to each other, smiled, and Marianne gave Mike a kiss. Johnny was already pushing the blue car to the start. Mike took his helmet, and gave Marianne a goodbye smile, crossing the first two fingers of his left hand for luck. Marianne replied with the same signal, and then went back to the Seven. She was going to watch the race with them.

Peter took the three walkie-talkie radios out of the bag he was carrying over his shoulder. 'George and Janet, here's yours!' he said, holding one of the sets out to his sister. 'You go up to the finish and then get straight in touch with us. Colin, you and Pam and Barbara take this one and go about half-way up the track. And Jack and I will stay here and let you know about the starting times.'

'You'd better hurry!' said Marianne. 'The first car starts in less than twenty minutes.'

The Seven separated, and went off in three different groups. It was quite a long way to walk to the finish, and George and Janet had hardly reached the foot of the stands facing the castle when Peter let them know the first driver was off. George started the stop-watch at once.

A little lower down the slope of the hill, at a bend where a bridle-path joined the road, Colin, Pam and Barbara were all looking at the second hands of their watches.

'One minute forty-six seconds!' said Colin, as the first car passed.

'Three minutes twelve seconds!' George announced, as it reached the finish.

Back at the start, Peter noted down the first driver's time, not forgetting to note his time at the half-way mark as well.

The black and white flag kept dipping. Colin and Pam and Barbara would see a car pass amidst clouds of dust soon afterwards, and a little later still, George and Janet noted another driver's finishing time.

As time went by, the more experienced competitors in the race were driving. After Number 25, the real contenders began coming up the track. Colin, Pam and Barbara had to draw back from their original position for safety's sake. The drivers were taking the hairpin bend where they stood at full speed now. Going at such a speed, the backs of their vehicles swerved off centre and brushed the bales of straw.

They saw Number 28 pass, and 29, and then 20, and then 21. And then, at last, Peter announced what all the children were eagerly awaiting.

'Calling from the start,' he said over the walkie-talkie. 'Mike's getting ready to go – his engine's roaring. Here it comes – the countdown's starting. Six, five, four, three, two, one . . . he's off! He's going like a bullet. Everyone here's shouting and applauding! He'll win – I'm sure he'll win!'

As the shouts of the crowd accompanied Mike along the track, Pam knew he couldn't be far away from where she and Colin and Barbara were standing at the half-way mark. She heard the noise coming closer. Then came the sound of the engine – and at last she saw it hurtling round the bend and coming straight on towards them, with the engine at full throttle.

Pam felt scared. How was Mike ever going to take the corner at such speed? Surely he'd crash into the barriers! However, he swung the car round – Colin could see the way its wheels swerved to keep it on course. Its back side-slipped, passing within a metre of the three children.

Now the car was racing down the short, straight section to the next bend, leaving a strong smell of burnt rubber behind it.

'It's the tyres – he took the bend so fast that the tyres overheated,' Colin explained.

'One minute thirty-four seconds!' said Barbara. Unlike Pam, she had kept quite cool, and remembered to time Mike to the half-way point.

'Oh, my goodness!' Pam suddenly exclaimed. She was watching Mike start round the next bend – he was dangerously near the place where the hillside dropped steeply away at the side of the road.

'It's all right – he's safely past that drop. Phew!' breathed Colin.

In the stands facing the castle, the crowd was

going wild. Everyone was shouting Mike's name and waving banners. George and Janet, feeling quite bemused, watched his triumphant finish.

'Two minutes fifty-nine seconds!' said George, once he had enough breath back to speak again!

It was certainly the best time anyone had made yet. Everybody realized that, and there was less interest in the next few drivers, who obviously weren't going to be as fast. Things became exciting again towards the end of this round, however, when the Italian, Giannini, was driving – he was timed at three minutes five seconds. Gonzalez, following him, didn't do very well on the gradient and turned in a rather mediocre time. At last the final car started – driven by Jimmy Curtis.

Colin felt butterflies in his tummy as he saw the American car come up the track like a red bullet. 'One minute twenty-four, one minute twenty-five, one minute twenty-six,' he counted breathlessly.

Was Curtis going to beat Mike? Surely not! Pam felt so nervous that she was chewing the ends of her blue scarf.

'One minute thirty, one minute thirty-one, one minute *thirty-two*!' said Colin, disappointed. 'He's made better time to the half-way mark than Mike.'

'Yes, Mike's time here was one minute thirty-four, wasn't it?' said Barbara gloomily.

'But Mike may still be leading!' Colin suddenly said, pointing up the track. Curtis was just taking the next bend. 'Look, he's skidding – he won't come out of the skid – '

'Oh no!' cried Pam, horrified.

But the car came to a halt, almost miraculously, on the very edge of the steep drop down the hillside. Only a little further and it would have gone over! Curtis started off again at once, but he had lost precious time.

Less than a minute later, George announced that he had passed the finishing line. 'Three minutes seven seconds!' he said.

So Mike was still in the lead. In fact, he was eight seconds ahead. The second round looked like being a real thriller!

Chapter Eleven

VICTORY!

There was half an hour's break in the race now, giving the drivers time to get back to the start. Watching the slow procession of cars, Colin, Pam and Barbara called good wishes to their friend as he passed, and Mike gave them a beaming smile.

'Well done, Mike!' shouted Barbara. 'We'll all soon be celebrating!'

Pam blew him a kiss, and Colin held up crossed fingers, just as he had seen Marianne do before the race started.

Down by the pits Peter and Jack were waiting for Mike. They had lost contact with Marianne and Johnny among the crowd. The first drivers were on their way down the track, and the mechanics were taking the cars to the petrol pumps and seeing their tanks were refilled.

Soon all the cars were back at the start and the track was clear again. Car Number 1 was ready to begin the second round.

'Four, three, two, one, zero!' And the chequered black and white flag came down. Off went the first car, to be followed by many others. This second round would take a good hour.

As the different teams waited for their turns, they were arguing among themselves – and the most heated argument of all was certainly going on in Jimmy Curtis's pit. Standing close to it, Susie and Binkie heard everything the driver himself was saying.

'I'd have cut his time by a couple of seconds but for that wretched bend!' Jimmy Curtis was saying. 'I changed down too late when I started on the hairpin there. I was doing five thousand r.p.m., and I'd have gone over the hillside if I hadn't braked!'

'Don't you fret, Jimmy,' Bob told him. 'Young Lee's not so sure of winning as all that! He'll come a cropper in the second round, you take my word for it!'

Overhearing this, Susie and Binkie winked at each other. They were delighted to hear what the American mechanic said – wouldn't they have loved to repeat it to the Seven, who were so keen for Mike Lee to win the race! Susie imagined Peter's face when he heard! It would just serve him right for not letting her join the Secret Seven Society. As if anyone would really *want* to be in it anyway, thought Susie, who *did*, despite Peter and Jack's explanation to her that they couldn't let anybody else join or it wouldn't be a Secret Seven any more.

And suddenly there *was* Peter, face to face with the two little girls, with Jack on his heels.

'Here's the silly old Secret Seven!' chanted Binkie mockingly.

'No – it's only the Terrible Two!' said Susie. 'They've lost the Feeble Five somewhere! I expect they don't want to see Mike Lee lose!'

'Mike's eight whole seconds ahead!' Jack told his sister. 'You'd better tell your friend Jimmy Curtis to drive a rocket next time, instead of a car!'

'That eight seconds won't do Mike Lee any good now,' said Susie triumphantly. 'He's going to come a cropper in this round – Bob said so!'

'Huh!' snorted Peter. 'We'll see about that.' And he and Jack walked on. In fact, the two boys had gone a little way before the full sense of what Susie had told them sank in.

'*Bob* said so!' cried Peter, horror-stricken. 'I don't like the sound of that one bit.'

'Nor do I,' Jack agreed. '*Bob* said he'd come a cropper in this round!'

'What do you bet he's sabotaged Mike's car in some way?' said Peter, all sorts of alarming possibilities occurring to him.

They began to run as fast as they could, making their desperate way through the crowd. They were quite close to the starting line, and could already see the black and white flag, when they heard the

loudspeakers announcing, 'Mike Lee to the start!
Mike Lee to the start! Countdown beginning: ten,
nine, eight, seven, six – '

'No!' yelled Peter, shoving past two spectators who
were standing in his way.

'Don't let him start!' shouted Jack, as loud as he
could.

'Three, two one, zero!'

The boys were too late. The car was off with a
tremendous roar.

Now what could they do? Peter kept his head and
snatched up his walkie-talkie. 'Hallo, Colin! Peter

here! Mike's just started. You've got to stop him –
listen, you've got to stop him somehow!'

'What?' Colin said incredulously into his own set.

'His car's been sabotaged!' yelled Peter frantically.

'Let's hope it's not too late!' said Jack.

A small crowd was gathering around the two boys.
'What's all this?' asked a couple of race officials.
'What are you talking about?'

'Where did you pick that information up?' asked
several reporters, hoping they were on the track of
a good story. But Peter didn't even hear their questions – he was waiting on tenter-hooks for Colin to
let him know what was happening.

Half-way up the track, at the bend where Pam,
Barbara and Colin were standing, some strange
things were going on. The alarmed spectators were
uttering exclamations of horror.

'Those kids will kill themselves!'

'The next car will go straight over the hillside!'

'Somebody ought to stop them!'

For the three children were on the track, shouting
and running. They had decided that the only thing
to do was to change Mike's course and thus slow
him down. As soon as the car just before him had
gone by, they jumped on to the track itself, knowing
they must act at once, and fast. With the speed of
panic, they moved away the bales of straw along the
side of the bend, opening up the junction with the
bridle path which went uphill into the wood. It was

a bit like switching the points on a railway line! Instead of taking the bend, Mike would have to carry straight on along the path, because the race track itself was now completely blocked off by bales.

Feeling desperate but quite fearless, Pam, Barbara and Colin clambered up on the bales of straw in the middle of the track themselves. When they saw Mike's car come round the bend lower down, they waved frantically to give their friend warning of the change to the track. But the blue car seemed to be coming closer and closer without slowing down at

all. Had Mike seen the three children? Did he understand what they were trying to tell him? The crowd were terrified for their safety.

On came the car. Colin, Pam and Barbara stayed where they were, pointing into the wood.

Mike was less than ten metres away now – less than five metres away! Was he going to turn, as he had been doing here ever since the practice sessions began?

No! He went straight on, the car jolting dangerously on the rough bridle path that led into the wood.

Colin and the two girls didn't waste a moment. They moved the bales of straw back to the side of the track, leaving the bend clear again – and just in time! They had hardly finished their work when the next car came shooting by.

It had been a close shave! But they didn't stop to think of all the awful things that might have happened. They ran after Mike.

He had managed to stop about a hundred metres along the bridle path. By the time the three children reached him he was getting out of the car, looking utterly baffled – and furious.

'You're crazy!' he cried, snatching off his helmet. 'What on earth got into you?'

Colin was about to explain how Peter had sent them a desperate message to stop him, when he noticed the left rear tyre of the car. 'You've got a flat tyre! It's completely flat!' he said, pointing.

Mike bent down at once to inspect the damage. To his great surprise he found an enormous nail driven right into the rubber of the tyre!

'But the track was carefully swept an hour before the race!' he said, bewildered. 'I just don't understand.'

Colin took the nail and examined it. 'Look – Made in USA,' he said triumphantly. 'It's stamped on the head of the nail.'

'Bob!' cried Pam. 'This must be Bob's doing!'

'He could have murdered you!' whispered Barbara, horrified.

And then Mike realized what danger he had been in. 'But for you, I'd be dead now, instead of standing here talking to you!' he said. 'It's impossible to keep control of the car with a flat tyre when you're going at such speeds. I'd have come to another bend and been unable to swing round, so I'd either have crashed into the hillside or gone over the edge.'

With tears in her eyes at this dreadful thought, Pam flung her arms round the driver and hugged him. 'But you're all right! You're alive!' she cried happily.

The race was going on, just as if nothing had happened, and when it came to Jimmy Curtis, driving last, he went over the track in excellent time, making up the full eight seconds he was behind Mike in the first round. So now he was in the lead. Everyone expected to see him given the victor's wreath on the rostrum opposite Malling Castle. But there had been much worried discussion among the race organizers when they heard the full story of what had happened to Mike Lee, and it was announced that he was to be allowed a second attempt. Rising to the challenge, Mike broke the record Curtis had just set in an incredible time of two minutes forty-three seconds!

Mr Fitzwilliam handed him the cup and victor's wreath, and he drove slowly back down the track, waving to the crowd as they applauded. George and Janet were with him, perched on the racing car's wings, and Colin, Pam and Barbara climbed up on the slowly moving vehicle too when it came to them.

Back at the starting line, Mike held out his victory wreath to Peter and Jack as they came hurrying up

to congratulate him. 'You won this race as much as I did!' he told them. 'In fact, it would have been my last race ever but for you!'

And Jimmy Curtis came over to congratulate Mike too. The American champion had been horrified to hear what Bob had done, and told Mike that he would make sure Bob never got any work in racing again. 'There's no place in the profession for dishonesty like that!' he said.

Marianne and Johnny joined them as well, and everyone was laughing and cheering. 'Hip, hip, hurray!'

'Three cheers for the Secret Seven!' called all the members of Mike's team. 'Well done, Secret Seven!'

'And three cheers for Susie and Binkie!' shouted Peter, to the amazement of his friends.

But of course he was quite right – but for their

talkative teasing, he would never have been warned of the danger threatening Mike Lee and his racing car.

So three cheers for Mike Lee, and three cheers for the Secret Seven, and three cheers for Susie and Binkie too! Hip, hip, hurray!

A complete list of the SECRET SEVEN ADVENTURES by Enid Blyton

KNIGHT BOOKS

**A complete list of new adventures about the
SECRET SEVEN**

KNIGHT BOOKS